Dear Parent:
Your child's love of reading

Every child learns to read in a different way and at his or her own speed. Some go back and forth between reading levels and read favorite books again and again. Others read through each level in order. You can help your young reader improve and become more confident by encouraging his or her own interests and abilities. From books your child reads with you to the first books he or she reads alone, there are I Can Read Books for every stage of reading:

SHARED READING
Basic language, word repetition, and whimsical illustrations, ideal for sharing with your emergent reader

BEGINNING READING
Short sentences, familiar words, and simple concepts for children eager to read on their own

READING WITH HELP
Engaging stories, longer sentences, and language play for developing readers

READING ALONE
Complex plots, challenging vocabulary, and high-interest topics for the independent reader

ADVANCED READING
Short paragraphs, chapters, and exciting themes for the perfect bridge to chapter books

I Can Read Books have introduced children to the joy of reading since 1957. Featuring award-winning authors and illustrators and a fabulous cast of beloved characters, I Can Read Books set the standard for beginning readers.

A lifetime of discovery begins with the magical words "I Can Read!"

Visit www.icanread.com for information
on enriching your child's reading experience.

HarperCollins®, 📖®, and I Can Read Book® are trademarks of HarperCollins Publishers.

Night at the Museum: Battle of the Smithsonian: To the Rescue!
Night at the Museum: Battle of the Smithsonian ™ and © 2009 Twentieth Century Fox Film Corporation. All Rights Reserved.
All rights reserved. Printed in the United States of America.
No part of this book may be used or reproduced in any manner whatsoever without written permission except
in the case of brief quotations embodied in critical articles and reviews. For information address HarperCollins Children's Books,
a division of HarperCollins Publishers, 1350 Avenue of the Americas, New York, NY 10019.
www.icanread.com

Library of Congress Catalog card number: 2008942540
ISBN 978-0-06-171558-7

Typography by Rick Farley

❖

First Edition

I Can Read!

READING
2
WITH HELP

NIGHT AT THE MUSEUM
BATTLE OF THE SMITHSONIAN
TO THE RESCUE!

Adapted by Catherine Hapka
Based on the screenplay by
Robert Ben Garant & Thomas Lennon

HarperCollins*Publishers*

Larry used to be the night guard
at the Museum of Natural History
in New York City.

He knew its biggest secret.

The statues came alive each night!

They were his friends.

Now Larry was a businessman.
He ran his own company
and made lots of money.
But he still visited the museum
whenever he had time.

One day, Larry's friends
were put into storage at the
Smithsonian Museum in Washington, D.C.
Larry had to rescue them!

First Larry borrowed a uniform.

He pretended he worked at the museum.

Then he looked for his friends.

He soon found them and the tablet

that brought them to life.

There was just one problem.

An old Egyptian king named Kahmunrah
wanted the magic tablet for himself.
"Give me that tablet!" he said.

Larry tried to escape from Kahmunrah on an old-fashioned motorcycle. He almost crashed into a woman, but skidded to a stop just in time. "What's the rumpus, Ace?" she asked.

The woman was Amelia Earhart.

"You might have heard of me.

I was the first woman

to cross the Atlantic," she said.

"What's your name, flyboy?"

"I'm Larry," Larry told Amelia.

Suddenly, spears flew at them.

Larry ran.

But Amelia wasn't afraid.

"Now we're going to have some fun!" she said.

Once they were safe,

Larry told Amelia about his mission.

Amelia wanted to help.

"I smell adventure, Mr. Daley,

and I want in!" Amelia said.

Larry and Amelia made their way

through the museum.

But they soon ran into trouble.

It was Napoleon!

He was helping Kahmunrah.

Napoleon took Larry prisoner

and dragged him to Kahmunrah.

Kahmunrah grabbed Larry's tablet.

"Behold!" he said.

"My evil army shall be set free!"

Kahmunrah tried to use the tablet

to open the gate to the Underworld.

But it didn't work!

"It's an old key," he grumbled.

"Sometimes you have to jiggle it."

Then Kahmunrah saw

the strange code on the tablet.

"You have one hour to find out

what the code means

or your friends will suffer,"

he said to Larry.

Larry told Amelia what had happened.

Luckily, Amelia had a plan.

Albert Einstein could help them!

They would go find him next door

at the Air and Space Museum.

Kahmunrah saw Larry and Amelia go.

He thought they were escaping,

so he sent his men after them.

Larry and Amelia ducked for cover.

While they hid, Amelia asked Larry
about his old job at the museum.
"Why did you leave?" she asked.
"Did you not like being a guard?"
"I loved it," Larry said sadly.

"You've lost your moxie,"

Amelia told Larry.

"I became a pilot for the fun of it.

Why else would anyone do anything?"

Finally, Amelia and Larry arrived
at the Air and Space Museum.

Einstein cracked the code in no time.

He was one of the smartest men ever!

"Got it," said Amelia.

Now Larry had to hurry back

to Kahmunrah and save his friends.

Amelia had an idea.

"Hop on, slowpoke," she said

as she jumped aboard a plane

built by the Wright Brothers.

Together they flew the plane

back to the other building.

It was time to stop the bad guys

once and for all!

Amelia led the charge

with the rest of Larry's friends

close behind.

Larry battled Kahmunrah.

The evil king was no match for him.

With one quick shove,

Larry sent Kahmunrah flying

back to the Underworld forever.

"Someone found his moxie,"

Amelia said proudly.

Larry realized it was true.

Now he knew what made him happy—

being a museum guard!

GET REAL!

Amelia Earhart was a real person.

Did you know ... ?

FACT Amelia was only the 16th woman to receive a pilot's license. She went on to break many flying records held by men.

FACT She was the first woman ever to cross the Atlantic Ocean in an airplane. The trip took her 20 hours and 40 minutes!

FACT Amelia influenced a lot of people, including Eleanor Roosevelt. Amelia even planned to teach the first lady how to fly!

FACT She began her flight around the world in June of 1937, but disappeared that same year. The United States government spent more than four million dollars searching for Amelia, but they never found her.